Once upon a time, there lived a poor merchant and his wife in a village. They used to perform menial tasks and run a small shop to make their livelihood. They were so poor that sometimes they had to ask for food from their neighbors.

One day, they decided to keep a duck to add to their income. They thought of selling the duck's eggs to make money.

So, they bought a duck from a neighboring village with all the meager money they had. They were unaware of the surprise that awaited them!

After some days, the duck laid two eggs. The merchant was amazed to see them! The eggs were truly Golden!!

Glistening and glittering, made of pure gold!! His happiness knew no bounds.

He excitedly took the golden eggs to his wife and informed her that he found them near the duck. Both of them jumped with joy. They decided to go to the market and sell the golden eggs.

They would make money out of them and use that money to expand their shop.

Now, the duck started laying a golden egg every day. The couple could not hold their happiness. They now had a lot of golden eggs. They stopped all the petty tasks they used to do for living.

They started selling the golden eggs and made huge money. Soon they were accustomed to living extravagantly without doing any work.

One day, the wife got a wicked idea. She asked her husband that why they should wait for a golden egg every day.

'Why can't we take all the eggs in the duck's stomach by killing it and make more money all at once?'

The foolish husband agreed to his wife's idea. The next night, they caught the duck and killed it mercilessly.

Sadly! All that they could find was blood. Not a single golden egg was found in the duck's stomach!

They both repented as they lost their only source of income. They learned a lesson that day, that greed is dangerous. It is only hard work and satisfaction that can bring happiness in true sense.

MORAL
Too much greed always leads to great loss.